For Braydon
and Mason—G. L.

Designed by Maureen Mulligan

Published by Disney Press, an imprint of Disney Book Group. No part of this book may be
reproduced or transmitted in any form or by any means, electronic or mechanical, including
photocopying, recording, or by any information storage and retrieval system, without written
permission from the publisher. For information address Disney Press, 1200 Grand Central
Avenue, Glendale, California 91201.
Printed in the United States of America
First Hardcover Edition, April 2018
1 3 5 7 9 10 8 6 4 2
FAC-034274-18047
ISBN 978-1-368-02461-7
Library of Congress Control Number: 2017954694
Visit www.disneybooks.com

The Magic is in You

By Colin Hosten and Brooke Vitale

Illustrated by Grace Lee

Disney PRESS

Los Angeles • New York

When the world around you seems

intimidating

and

dangerous,

just *remember* . . .

The *magic* is in you . . .

to spread love and

inspire

others.

When life gets so complicated you don't know
what to do next, it's okay to cry.

Just **remember** . . .

The *magic* is in you . . .

to honor your

feelings

and trust your

inner voice.

Sometimes life comes at you so fast
that all you can do is run.

Just remember . . .

The *magic* is in you . . .

to confront your

challenges

and

discover

your

strengths.

When the future seems uncertain and you don't know where to go next,

just remember...

The **magic** is in you . . .

to
persevere
and achieve your dreams.

When relationships are tested by
trials and tribulations,

just remember . . .

The **magic** is in you . . .

to reveal the

power

of true

friendship.

Growing up can sometimes make
you feel awkward

and

alone.

Just remember . . .

The **magic** is in you . . .

to celebrate
yourself and
soar.

It's hard to leave the
past behind.

Just remember ...

The **magic** is in you . . .

to embrace
a future of
beautiful
memories.

Above all, when your dreams seem

out of reach,

just remember . . .

The *magic* is in

YOU

to do the

impossible.